An I Can Read Book®

SPOOKY TRICKS

by Rose Wyler and Gerald Ames
pictures by S. D. Schindler

HarperTrophy
A Division of HarperCollinsPublishers

With thanks to
the many young
ghosts who helped us

—R.W. & G.A.

I Can Read Book is a registered trademark of
HarperCollins Publishers.

SPOOKY TRICKS
Text copyright © 1968, 1994 by Rose Wyler and Gerald Ames
Illustrations copyright © 1994 by Steven D. Schindler
Printed in the U.S.A.   All rights reserved.
Revised and Newly Illustrated Edition

Library of Congress Cataloging-in-Publication Data
Wyler, Rose.
   Spooky tricks / by Rose Wyler and Gerald Ames ; pictures by S. D.
Schindler.
      p.   cm. — (An I can read book)
   "A newly illustrated edition."
   Summary: Describes how to write invisible messages, make ghosts appear
on walls, and many other tricks.
   ISBN 0-06-023025-8. — ISBN 0-06-023026-6 (lib. bdg.)
   ISBN 0-06-444172-5 (pbk.)
   1. Conjuring—Juvenile literature.   [1. Magic tricks.]   I. Ames, Gerald.
II. Schindler, S. D., ill.   III. Title.   IV. Series.
GV1548.W86   1994   92-47501
793.8—dc20   CIP
                                                        AC

First Harper Trophy edition, 1994.
❖

CONTENTS

How to Be a Ghost   4

Willie the Ghost   23

Haunted House   41

HOW TO BE
A GHOST

The night is dark

and shadows creep around.

This is a night of ghosts

and scary magic.

Who will do the magic?

You will.

You will do spooky tricks

and scare everyone, even yourself.

Are you ready?

ARE YOU A REAL GHOST?

Do you have holes like a real ghost?

Let's find out with a magic X ray.

Roll up a sheet of paper

to make a tube.

Hold up one hand beside the tube.

Look through the tube with one eye,

but keep your other eye open.

It looks like your hand has a hole!

Wow! You are a real ghost.

YOUR PHANTOM FINGER

Did you know you have an extra finger

floating around in the air?

Hold your two first fingers

a little in front of your eyes.

Look past them toward the wall.

What's floating before you?

A finger with a nail at each end!

This is your phantom finger.

SPOOKY HAND

Place your hand flat on the table.

Push a card under it, then another,

until ten cards are under your hand.

Say, "Hocus-pocus,"

and slowly lift your hand.

The cards come up with your hand!

The trick: Put on a loose ring.

Push a toothpick under it.

The toothpick holds

the first card,

and it holds the others.

STRANGE STRING

Say, "Only a ghost can make

these two strings become one."

Put the upper ends into your mouth.

Let the other ends hang down.

Chew the string.

Make faces and roll your eyes.

Take a hanging end and pull it.

The string is in one long piece!

The secret: Loop a long string

with a very short one.

Hide the loop with your thumb,

then put it into your mouth.

Keep the short string in your mouth.

Pull out the long one.

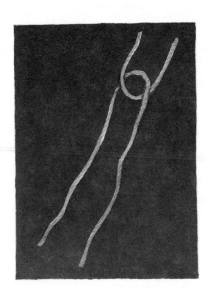 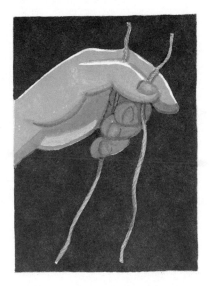

SPOOKY HANDKERCHIEF

Say, "My handkerchief is so spooky,

a coin will pass through it."

Hold up a coin

between your finger and thumb.

14

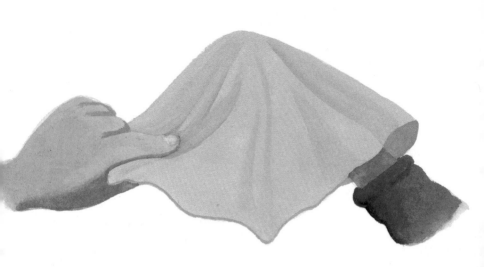

Cover it with your handkerchief.

Pinch the handkerchief

between your thumb and the coin.

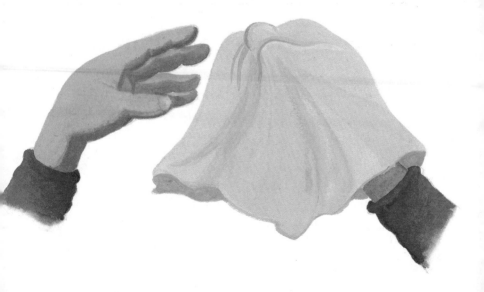

Flip the handkerchief back

to show that the coin is still there.

Then flip it forward.

The coin seems to be in the fold,

but it is really *behind* the fold.

16

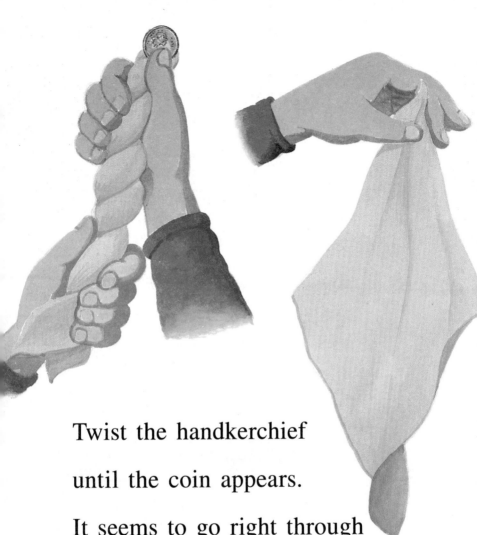

Twist the handkerchief

until the coin appears.

It seems to go right through

the handkerchief.

Then unfold the handkerchief.

There is no hole!

RISING RING

Say, "My ring can move by itself."

Drop the ring over a pencil.

Say, "Rise, spooky ring, rise."

The ring slowly rises.

Then it falls and rises again.

The trick: Take a black thread.

Tie one end to your coat button.

Fix the other end under the eraser.

No one will see the thread.

When you lean back,

the thread pulls tight

and makes the ring rise.

Lean forward and the ring falls.

X-RAY EYES

Say, "I will use my X-ray eyes

to read through folded paper."

Tell your friends, "Spell your name,

and I will write it down."

Put each name on a sheet of paper.

Fold each sheet

and drop them all in a bag.

Ask someone to pick out a sheet.

Stare at the folded paper. Then say,

"I see that the name is John."

When the paper is unfolded,

the name on it is "John."

The trick: Pick one name—

suppose it is John—

and write that name on every sheet.

WILLIE THE GHOST

Say, "Sometimes I need a helper

for my spooky tricks.

I have a good helper.

He is a small ghost named Willie.

Do you want to meet him?"

WILLIE WRITES
A MESSAGE

Call in a loud voice,

"Willie, Willie, do you hear me?

Write a message

on this sheet of paper."

Then pick up the paper and say,

"Let us see what Willie wrote."

Hold the paper above a toaster
and warm it carefully.

Slowly Willie's words appear:

"I AM A GOOD GHOST."

The trick: Before the show,
write the message with lemon juice.

Use a pen or a toothpick.

WILLIE IN A MATCHBOX

Say, "Willie is so little,

he sleeps in a matchbox."

Lay the matchbox on your hand.

Say, "Willie, it's time to get up."

Slowly bend your fingers down.

The matchbox rises and stands up.

"Now it's time for bed, Willie."

Straighten your fingers,

and the box lies down.

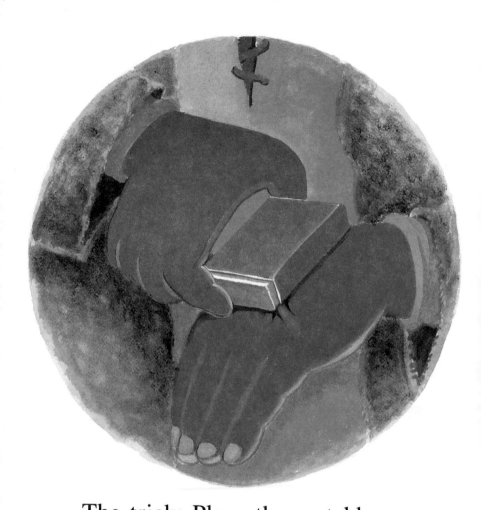

The trick: Place the matchbox

upside down on your hand.

Pinch a little skin

between the box and the cover.

28

WILLIE PLAYS BALL

Put a ball on the table and say,

"Willie likes to play ball.

Willie, give the ball a push."

The ball moves back and forth.

29

The trick: Tie a thread to a ring.

Place the ring under the tablecloth.

Run the thread over

and under the tabletop.

Put the ball on the ring.

When you pull the thread,

the ring moves the ball.

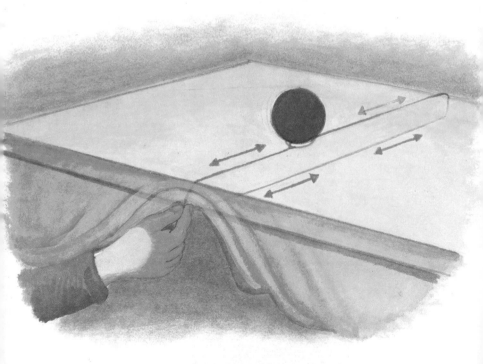

WILLIE EARNS A NICKEL

Say, "Willie, here is a nickel
for you.
First I will shine it."
Rub the nickel on your sleeve.
Drop the nickel and pick it up.

Rub it some more.

Hold out your hand and say,

"Here is your nickel, Willie."

Then show that your hand is empty.

Your other hand is empty too.

Willie took his nickel!

The trick: When you drop the nickel,
pick it up with one hand.
Keep it there, but pretend
to shift it to the other hand.
Hold out the empty hand and
slip the nickel into your shirt.

WILLIE TIES A KNOT

Take one corner of a handkerchief.

Say, "I will tie a knot by magic."

Then lift the lower corner

and hold it in the same hand.

Flip the handkerchief

so it hangs down as before.

No knot appears.

Too bad!

You try again.

Still no knot appears.

"Oh, dear!" you say.

"I need Willie.

Willie, help me.

Please tie a knot."

Flip the handkerchief once more and—

a knot appears in the lower corner!

35

The trick: Tie a knot in one corner
of the handkerchief.

Hold this corner so you hide the knot.

When you want the knot to appear,

let the knotted corner drop down.

CREEPY COIN

Stand a glass upside down

on two nickels

with a dime between them.

Say, "Willie, bring the dime to me."

Scratch on the tablecloth.

The dime comes out

from under the glass!

The scratching moves the dime.

38

CANDY FOR WILLIE

Hold up a paper cup

so the bottom rests on your palm.

Put a piece of candy in the cup.

Say, "Here, Willie, take your candy."

Cover the cup with a handkerchief.

Then uncover it

and turn the cup upside down.

The candy is gone!

The trick: Make a hole

in the bottom of the cup

so the candy drops into your hand.

HAUNTED HOUSE

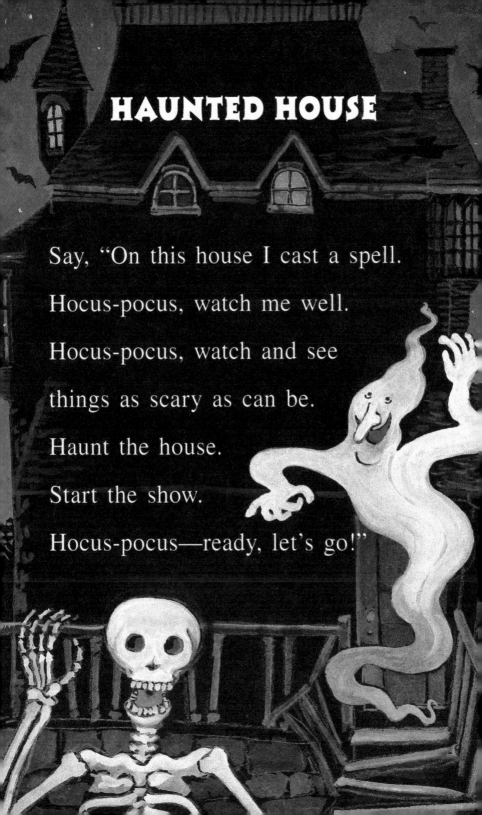

Say, "On this house I cast a spell.

Hocus-pocus, watch me well.

Hocus-pocus, watch and see

things as scary as can be.

Haunt the house.

Start the show.

Hocus-pocus—ready, let's go!"

ELECTRIC CAT

Show your cat and say,
"I had a spooky kitten
who became a spooky cat.
She sparkles in the dark.
What do you think of that!"
Turn out the lights.

The sparks jump up
around your spooky cat.
The trick: Use a long-haired cat.
Run a comb through the cat's fur.
This will charge the fur
with electricity.

GHOST ON THE WALL

Draw a large picture of a ghost.

Make it black with white eyes.

Tell your friends to stare

at the picture for a minute.

Then say, "Stare at the wall."

What do they see?

They see the ghost,

but now it is white.

Their own eyes play a trick on them.

SIGN OF THE GHOST

Show a lump of sugar and a pencil.

Write the letter "G" on the sugar.

Then drop it into a glass of water.

Say, "Sugar, melt.

Letter 'G,' float up."

Hold a friend's hand over the glass.

Then tell him to look at his hand.

There on his palm is the "G."

It is the sign of the ghost!

The trick: Press your finger

on the "G" on the sugar.

The "G" comes off on your finger.

When you show your friend

what to do, hold his hand

and touch his palm with your finger.

This puts the "G" on his palm.

DISAPPEARING GIRL

Show a large cardboard box and say,

"Will a brave girl please come here?

I will make you disappear."

Sue is brave.

Sue steps into the box.

Put down the cover,

wave your hands,

and say some magic words.

Then tip the box forward

and lift the cover.

The box is empty!

This is how you fix the box:

Cut around the bottom on three sides.

Bend the bottom toward the front

and put a handle on the bottom.

When Sue steps into the box,

she is standing on the floor.

51

As you tip the box forward,

she pulls the bottom back.

When you lift the cover,

she is hidden behind the box.

How does Sue know what to do?

She practiced and practiced

the trick with you.

MUMMY FINGER

Say, "What do I have in this box?

A mummy's finger I found in Egypt.

Do not faint now."

Open the box.

It is packed with cotton.

Push aside the cotton and—

there is the mummy's finger!

The trick: It is your own finger.

You poke it into the box

through a hole in the bottom.

54

MIXED-UP MUMMIES

Show two matchboxes

and two paper-doll mummies.

One mummy is purple.

The other is green.

Put the purple mummy in a box.

Mark the end of that box

with a purple "X."

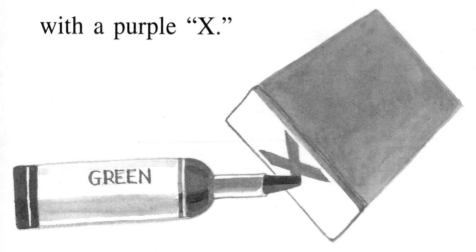

Put the green mummy in the other box.

Mark the end with a green "X."

Cover the boxes with a cloth.

Then uncover and open them.

The mummies have changed places!

Before the trick,

mark a green "X"

on the purple mummy's box.

Mark a purple "X"

on the green mummy's box.

Keep these ends out of sight.

As you uncover the boxes,

turn them around so these ends show.

FLOATING BOY

Say, "For my last surprise,

a boy will float before your eyes."

A low bench is covered with a sheet.

Two helpers stand waiting.

Who will be the floating boy?

A friend comes up—

suppose his name is Tom.

He stands behind the bench.

Your two helpers take the sheet.

They hold it up before the bench.

Tom is hidden behind the sheet.

He lies down on the bench.

The helpers cover him with the sheet.

Only his head and feet show.

Wave your hands over Tom.

Say, "Rise! Rise!"

Tom floats up into the air!

How the trick works:

Two sticks with shoes on the ends

are hidden under the sheet.

When Tom lies down,

he knows what to do.

He keeps his feet on the floor

and takes hold of the two sticks.

As Tom slowly stands up,

he lifts the sticks.

Take off the sheet,

and everybody laughs.

The spell is broken.

The ghosts all go.

This is the end

of the spooky tricks show.